PowerKids Readers:
My World of Science™

Pulleys in My World

Joanne Randolph

The Rosen Publishing Group's
PowerKids Press™
New York

For Linda Lou and Lucas

Published in 2006 by The Rosen Publishing Group, Inc.
29 East 21st Street, New York, NY 10010

First Edition

Book Design: Julio Gil

Photo Credits: Cover and p. 9 (flag) by Maura B. McConnell; Cover (crane) © Arthur S. Aubry/Getty Images; Cover (well) © Andrew Cowin; Travel Ink/Corbis; p. 5 © James P. Blair/Corbis; pp. 7, 19, 22 (crane), 22 (groove) by Cindy Reiman; p. 11 © Ric Ergenbright/Corbis; p. 13 © Bob Krist/Corbis; p. 15 © Digital Vision/Getty Images; p. 17 © Marc Garanger/Corbis; p. 21 © Royalty-Free/Corbis; p. 22 (blinds) Photodisc Green/Getty Images; p. 22 (laundry) © Tim McGuire/Corbis; p. 22 (well) © Eric and David Hosking/Corbis; p. 22 (window) © David Papazian/Corbis.

Library of Congress Cataloging-in-Publication Data

Randolph, Joanne.
  Pulleys in my world / Joanne Randolph.— 1st ed.
      p. cm. — (My world of science)
  Includes bibliographical references and index.
  ISBN 1-4042-3308-3 (library binding)
  1. Pulleys—Juvenile literature. I. Title.
TJ1103.R36 2006
621.8'11—dc22
                                                2005005974

Manufactured in the United States of America

Contents

People use simple machines to help them do work. A pulley is one kind of simple machine. It can be used to lift and move heavy objects.

5

A pulley looks like a wheel with a groove. A rope can be passed around this wheel. Something fixed to one side of the rope can be lifted by a person pulling on the other side.

rope

wheel

groove

7

A flag on a flagpole uses a pulley. The pulley is fixed to the top of the pole. A rope goes around the pulley. The flag is put on the rope. The flag can be moved up or down the pole using the rope.

Have you ever seen a well? People use wells to get water that is under the ground. A well uses a pulley to help people lift the water from the bottom of the well.

Some people hang their clothes on a line to dry. This line can be attached to a pulley. The person moves the laundry by pulling on the rope. This makes hanging clothes easier.

pulley

13

Your home may have coverings over the windows called blinds. Blinds are raised by pulling a rope attached to a pulley.

A dumbwaiter uses a pulley to lift things, too. A dumbwaiter is a simple elevator. It can be used to move heavy things from one floor to another.

Have you ever seen a crane? Cranes are used for jobs like putting up buildings. Cranes have a tall arm that is used to lift heavy things. At the top of the arm is a pulley.

Can you think of pulleys you see around you? Look at this picture. Can you find the pulleys here?

Words to Know

blinds   crane

groove   laundry

well   window

Here are more books to read about pulleys in your world:
What Is a Pulley? (Welcome Books) by Lloyd G. Douglas Children's Press, 2002

Web Sites:
Due to the changing nature of Internet links, PowerKids Press has developed an online list of Web sites related to the subject of this book. This site is updated regularly. Please use this link to access the list:
www.powerkidslinks.com/mws/pulleys/

Index

Word Count: 278

Note to Librarians, Teachers, and Parents
PowerKids Readers are specially designed to help emergent and beginning readers build their skills in reading for information. Sentences are short and simple, employing a basic vocabulary of sight words, simple vocabulary, and basic concepts, as well as new words that describe objects or processes that relate to the topic. Large type, clean design, and stunning photographs corresponding directly to the text all help children to decipher meaning. Features such as a contents page, picture glossary, and index introduce children to the basic elements of a book, which they will encounter in their future reading experiences.